I WISH IT WOULD SNOW!

Sarah Dillard

Aladdin

NEW YORK   LONDON   TORONTO   SYDNEY   NEW DELHI

To my friends at Mad River Glen. Think snow!

ALADDIN
An imprint of
Simon & Schuster
Children's Publishing Division · 1230
Avenue of the Americas, New York, New York 10020
· First Aladdin hardcover edition December 2018 ·
Copyright © 2018 by Sarah Dillard
All rights reserved, including the right of reproduction in whole or
in part in any form. · ALADDIN and related logo are registered trademarks
of Simon & Schuster, Inc. · For information about special discounts for bulk
purchases, please contact Simon & Schuster Special Sales at 1-866-506-1949 or
business@simonandschuster.com. · The Simon & Schuster Speakers Bureau can bring authors to your
live event. For more information or to book an event contact the Simon & Schuster Speakers
Bureau at 1-866-248-3049 or visit our website at www.simonspeakers.com. · Book designed
by Laura Lyn DiSiena · The illustrations for this book were rendered digitally. · The text of this
book was hand-lettered. · Manufactured in China 0918 SCP · 10 9 8 7 6 5 4 3 2 1
Library of Congress Control Number 2018943441
ISBN 978-1-5344-0676-6 (hc)
ISBN 978-1-5344-0677-3 (eBook)

I want it  to snow.

Please   let it snow.

I need it to

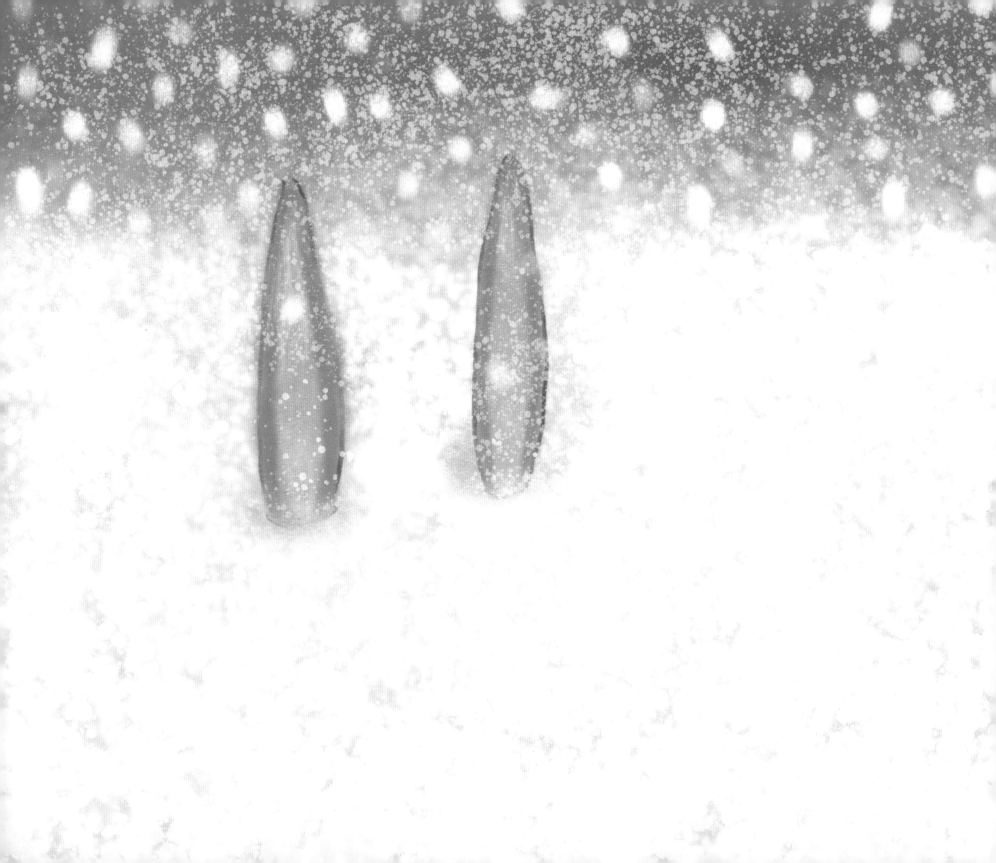

Too much snow.

I wish it would stop.   I want it to stop.

Please make it stop.

I need it to . . .

Ohhh!